Shane McG

Anyone for Tennis?

To Paulipops – Remember to bend your knees!

PIPPBROOK BOOKS

First published in the UK in 2007 by Templar Publishing.
This edition published in the UK in 2016 by Pippbrook Books,
an imprint of The Templar Company Limited,
part of the Bonnier Publishing Group,
The Plaza, 535 King's Road, London, SW10 0SZ
www.templarco.co.uk
www.bonnierpublishing.com

Copyright © 2007 by Shane McG

1 3 5 7 9 10 8 6 4 2

All rights reserved

ISBN 978-1-78370-561-0

Designed by Mike Jolley
Edited by Stella Gurney

Printed in Malaysia

PIPPBROOK
BOOKS

Hi. I'm Tom Foley...

and I'm 7 years of age.

I know this because yesterday was my birthday and I got lots of great presents.

They're all brilliant and do lots of amazing stuff like BEEP and CRASH and WHIRR.

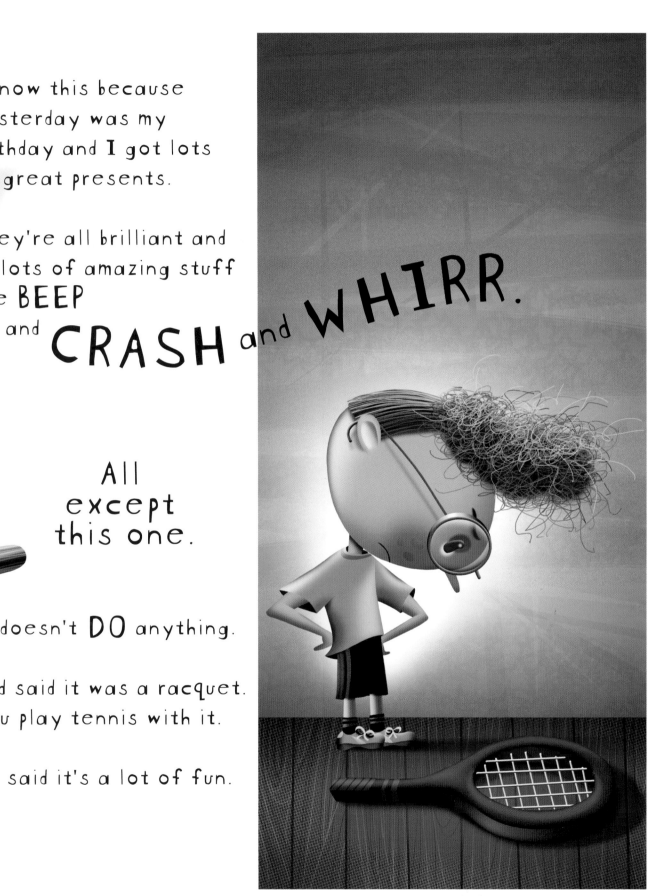

All except this one.

It doesn't DO anything.

Dad said it was a racquet. You play tennis with it.

He said it's a lot of fun.

I wasn't convinced.

"WHO PLAYS TENNIS?"

I asked Dad.

My sister Ida doesn't play tennis.
In fact she doesn't do ANYTHING.

(Except lie in her bedroom all day
talking to her friend Tania about
boys and shopping.)

How boring is that?

"WHO PLAYS TENNIS?

Mum doesn't play tennis.

All she wants to do is stand on one leg humming and doing her yoghurt."

"I think you mean yoga," Dad said.

Whatever.

It looks dumb.

"SO WHO PLAYS TENNIS?"

My cat Smudgy doesn't play tennis.

She spends her entire day **eating**...

and passing wind.

"PHEW! Smudgy!"

My Best Friend Kevin doesn't play tennis either.

He spends all his time riding his lovely new green bike.

Without giving me a turn.

EVER.

Actually he's my Sixth-Best Friend.

And my dog Spike definitely doesn't play tennis.

He's way too busy chasing cars.

Poor ol' Spike. He never catches them.

My cuddly blue croc **certainly** doesn't play tennis.

That would be crazy!

He'd trip over the ball.

I don't think he was listening.

He was too

busy...

...hitting balls at me. I had to duck for cover.
I thought about running away but I'm not a scaredy cat.

"Don't worry," Dad said.

"When I hit the ball to you,
you hit it back to me.

Then I'll hit it back to you.

Then you hit it back to me.

Okay?"

"Okay."

I took a really **BIG** swing at the ball...

and fell over!

"You just need a little practice,"
said Dad.

...AND PRACTISE

is just what I did!

On the way home Dad asked me,
"Who plays tennis, son?"

I said, "That's easy-peasy, Dad.

TOM FOLEY PLAYS TENNIS!"

My racquet is **pretty cool** after all.

It doesn't beep or crash or whirr
but you **CAN** play **TENNIS** with it...